For
Maria & Kitty

First published in the United States 1997
by Dial Books for Young Readers
A Division of Penguin Books USA Inc.
375 Hudson Street
New York, New York 10014

Published in Great Britain 1997
by Reed Children's Books
Copyright © 1997 by Belinda Downes
Printed in China
First Edition
1 3 5 7 9 10 8 6 4 2

Library of Congress Cataloging in Publication Data
Downes, Belinda.
Every little angel's handbook / by Belinda Downes.—1st ed.
p. cm.
Summary: Tells how angels dress, play, work, cook,
and learn to do their jobs properly.
ISBN 0-8037-2264-8 [1. Angels–Fiction.] I. Title.
PZ7.D7577Ev 1997 [E]–dc21 96-50158 CIP AC

Every
Little Angel's
Handbook

words and embroideries by
Belinda Downes

Dial Books for Young Readers · New York

Angels are around us at all times.
You may not see them, but they certainly see you.
And they don't just sit around on clouds all day.
Angels have work to do, people to visit, and
messages to deliver. They have rainbows to paint,
stars to polish, and snow to make.

Little angels have to learn to fly and sing
and shoot arrows and make angel cakes.
And most important, they have to learn to
look and behave like real angels.

If you are considering becoming a little angel,
read carefully and you will learn everything
you need to know.

Gabriella

Angelica

Gloria

Eric

Mabel

Bob

All little angels need guidance. They must learn special skills for their important work. The older, wiser angels are in charge of day-to-day activities and teaching the younger angels.

Peter

Lucy

Ariel

John Francis

Tabitha

Valentino

Some can be a little serious, but most of the older angels
like to have fun, and they are *all* kind and full of understanding.
These are some of the angels in charge. You will see what they do later in the book.

Angel Style

Angels can be very fussy about their appearances and they
certainly don't all wear white.

Icing Sugar Summer Firebird

Rainbow Traditional Midnight

From the plain and humble traditional look to something for a special
angelic occasion, angels can choose from their very own style catalogue.
Even the most fashion conscious will find the perfect outfit.

Choosing accessories to match is just as easy.
Not all angels have dainty feet.
Eight out of ten guardian angels prefer sturdy boots in case they
have to help little devils mind their own business.

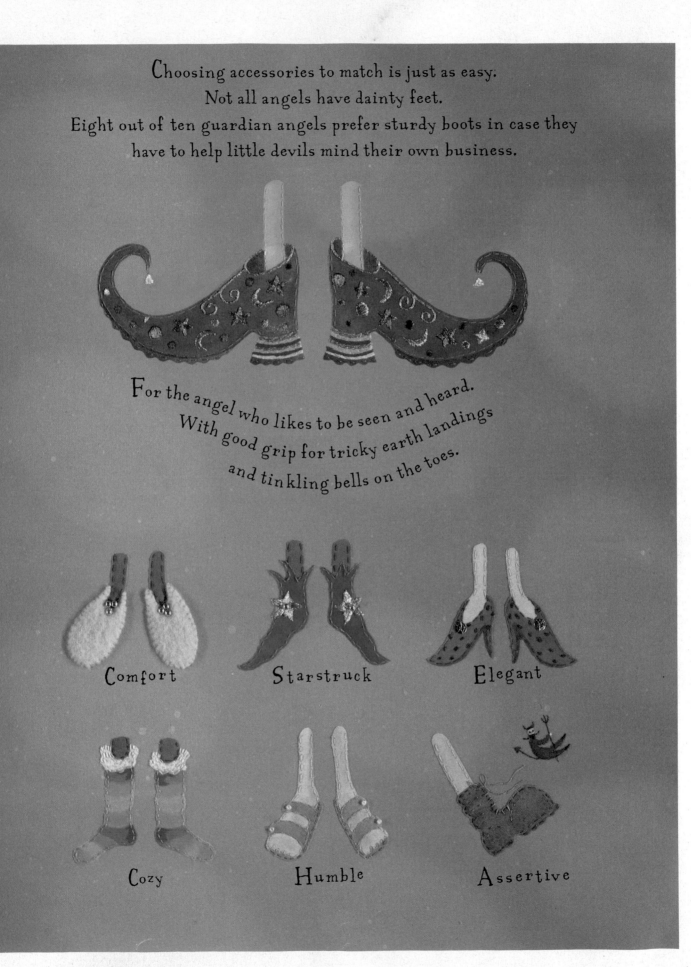

For the angel who likes to be seen and heard.
With good grip for tricky earth landings
and tinkling bells on the toes.

Comfort   Starstruck   Elegant

Cozy   Humble   Assertive

Angel Florence is sporting a Basic hairstyle, and modelling the Firebird robe with a pair of Elegant shoes and the Stardust bag.

Even hairstyles come in all shapes and sizes.
Some are easy to manage, but others—
such as Lightning—cause havoc in the skies.

Romantic

Cupid Curl

Basic

Lightning

Crazy Curl

Roly Poly

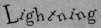

Bags are useful for carrying stardust, angel feathers,
wing spray, star polish, emergency supplies of vanishing powder,
and notebooks filled with long lists of things to do.

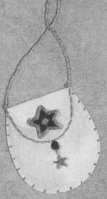
Stellar

Stardust

Starburst

Exotic

Golden Cloud

Regal

Go-Lightly

Sunlight

Earth

Dazzler

Of course, every little angel needs wings and a halo—and not basic ones either.
Large, small, feathery, curvy, pointed, patterned, frosted, gold, silver,
or see-through, the selection is endless. It could take an age to choose.

Fixing Stars With Eric

Eric works in the star department.
His robe of night blue allows him to fly unseen
through the starry night skies.
His soft, curly toed shoes are practical and easy to wear.
Stars need a lot of care and must be
taken down, cleaned, and put back in place before
the people on earth notice.

Eric and his friends polish stars with magic stardust
and spend most nights chasing shooting stars
and catching falling ones.
His dark glasses are useful when unexpected stars whizz by,
sparkling and fizzing with tails of bright lights.

Making Snowflakes With Mabel

Mabel works for the snow and ice department.
She makes frost, ice, hailstones, and snowflakes.
It's cold work, but her Fluffy Cloud robe keeps her warm.
The most difficult part is cutting out snowflakes so that each one
has a unique pattern.
Only the most patient angels are chosen to do this.

Learning to Cook With Angelica

Angelica Pudding teaches cooking.
When everyone is baking, complete concentration is needed.
Angelica's cakes are always light and fluffy and
taste delicious—if you can catch one.

But when Angelica isn't looking, the little angels
are mischievous. They squirt icing at each other,
spill flour, and throw cake mixture down to earth.
Teaching angels to cook is a messy business,
but there has not been a bad angel cake yet!

Singing in the Choir With Gloria

Gloria, the choir mistress, is very patient.
(She makes snowflakes on her days off.)
The little angels often sing wrong notes or even
completely different songs, but amazingly Gloria always remains calm.
She taps her conductor's baton and they just sing more.

They need lots of practice if they are ever to reach heavenly standards
and sing at special angelic events.

Flying Lessons

The problem with learning to fly is that the little angels get overexcited and fly too far and too fast before they are ready.

Having strong wings is the most important part of flying, but they need constant care and repair.

The flight instructor, Ariel, teaches takeoff, landing, and perfect wing control before he allows any fancy flying.

Patching up holes is never enough.
Expert angels stitch, glue, and repaint tired wings.

Weather Angels

Angels try to plan the weather in advance, but it doesn't always turn out as they expect. Sometimes everything gets muddled, the angels get confused, and one minute it's raining and the next it's sunny. Angels like summer best, when they can flit and float on gentle breezes.

Guardian Angels

Gabriella is in charge of the guardian angels. They are kept
busy making sure the people on earth don't get into trouble,
lose things, or have accidents.
It's not easy to take a vacation when you're a guardian angel!

Cupid Angels

Cupids really enjoy lying around on clouds all day and can be very lazy. The cupid leader, Angel Valentino, has to remind them that falling in love is a serious business and that their arrows should not hit the wrong people.

Special Effects

Angels Bob and John Francis are a good team when it comes to organizing special effects in the heavens. Red skies at night, eclipses, comets, and shooting stars are among their favorites. Only angels like Bob and John Francis who have passed their advanced flying test can put stars and other bright lights in the sky.

As the world turns around and around, day becomes night and night becomes day. Angels are always busy; dawn to dusk to dawn again. Flying over the earth they have the best view of the world, and as we sleep they wish us well and send us messages in our dreams.

DATE DUE
